A Scary Tale

A Scary Tale

First Edition 8/2021

Helpful Little Books

www.helpful-little-books.com

Suzy Squirrel woke up and stretched.
Today was going to be a good day,
she thought to herself.

Suzy looked out of her drey.
She was so excited.
She was going to meet
her friends for a play date.

Suzy's Mum had made breakfast. She was about
to go foraging for food and said,
"Suzy please wash your bowl and spoon
before you go off to play."

Her Mum also asked Suzy to be back home before it was dark but Suzy wasn't really listening and just munched on her breakfast thinking about what a great day she was going to have.

No sooner had Mum left
than Suzy heard some voices,
"Hey Suzy, are your ready!"
She looked out and saw her
friends Stuart the Stoat and
Rachel the Rabbit
waiting at the bottom of
the tree.
Suzy looked back at
her dirty bowl and spoon,
"Erm, I've got to..." but
Suzy wanted to play
so she scampered down the tree to
join her friends.

The three friends ran towards the wide open space of the meadow.

They played games, chased each other around and generally messed about, without a care in the world.

Soon the sun was setting and it was also getting rather cloudy.

"I need to go home," said Stuart the Stoat.
"Oh come on, just one more game," replied Suzy.
"Sorry I've got to go as well" said Rachel the Rabbit.

"You can take a short cut through the woods," suggested Suzy, pointing at the dark trees next to the meadow.

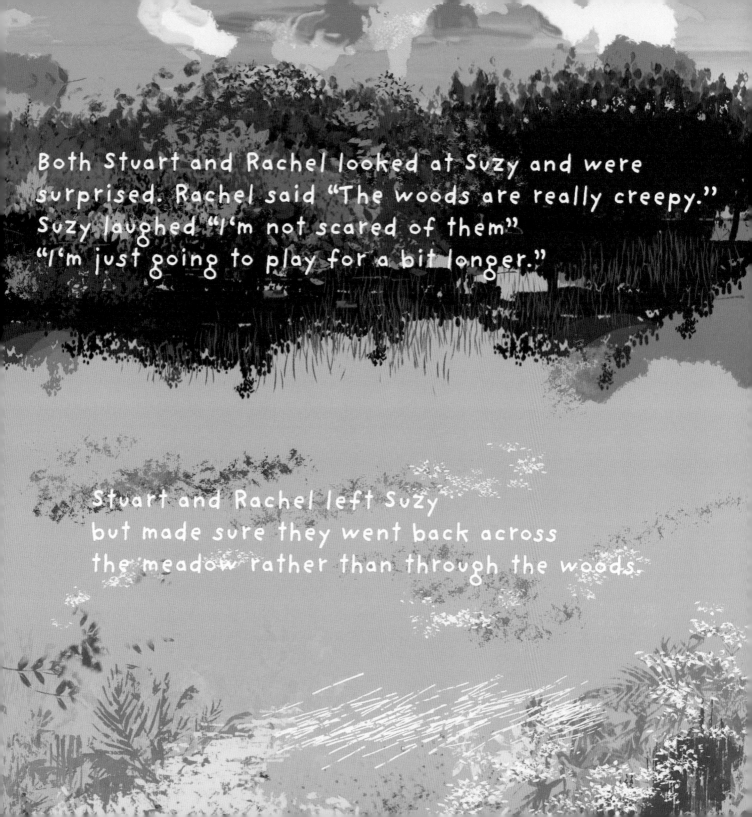

Both Stuart and Rachel looked at Suzy and were
surprised. Rachel said "The woods are really creepy."
Suzy laughed "I'm not scared of them"
"I'm just going to play for a bit longer."

Stuart and Rachel left Suzy
but made sure they went back across
the meadow rather than through the woods.

Suzy carried on playing and made a pretty daisy chain. Just then she felt a drop of rain land on her head.

Suzy looked up. Big, grey clouds were swirling above and she heard a low rumble of thunder.

Suzy was worried, so she started to head back across
the meadow but suddenly the rain began to pour.
She was going to get soaked and needed to get
home quickly.

KEEP OUT

She looked back towards the woods.
They seemed dark and a little bit scary
but she knew it would be a faster way home
plus the trees might shelter her from the rain.

Suzy entered the woods and by now the rain was falling heavily and the wind was blowing through the trees making them swirl and sway.

Suzy moved along as quickly as she could. Just then there was a big flash of lightning that created shadows in the woods. Suzy thought she saw a big shape moving with her.

She looked around but there was nothing there.

CRACK! BOOM!

Suzy's heart was pounding from running but she was scared as well and really regretted taking the short cut.

WHOOSH!

Another flash of lightning and Suzy saw
the big shadow moving with her.
Again she looked around but there was
no sign of anything.

Suzy ran as fast as she could through the trees.

FLASH!

There was yet another bright streak of lightning and Suzy again saw the big shadow that seemed to be following her.

CRACK -BOOM-ROAR

The thunder rang out again.
She was very scared indeed.

WHOOSH!

Another flash of lightning and
Suzy saw the big shadow still moving
with her, so she ran even faster.

She imagined she was being chased by a big bear or a hungry lion or maybe even a snake. "Please let me get home," "Please let me get home," she muttered to herself.

Just then she heard a voice calling for her,
"Suzy! Where are you!"

It was her Mum who was very worried and
had come to look for Suzy. "I'm here Mum!"
Suzy shouted.

WHOOSH!

Another flash of lightning and there was
the big shadow again, almost on top of her.

CRACK-BOOM-BOOM!

Again the thunder rang out. She looked around
but there was still nothing there.

THUD!

Suzy ran into something,
she looked up and there was
her mum.
"Quickly, let's get home,"
she said.

Back at the drey, Suzy's Mum was drying her head with a towel. "I was being followed by something big and scary,"

Suzy looked up and saw a huge shadow on the wall of the drey. Suzy shouted, "Agh! It's here!"

Her mum looked around and saw the shadow on the wall then laughed.

"What's so funny!" Suzy asked. "That's my tail, watch."
Her Mum wiggled her bushy tail and the shadow
behind her moved along at the same time.

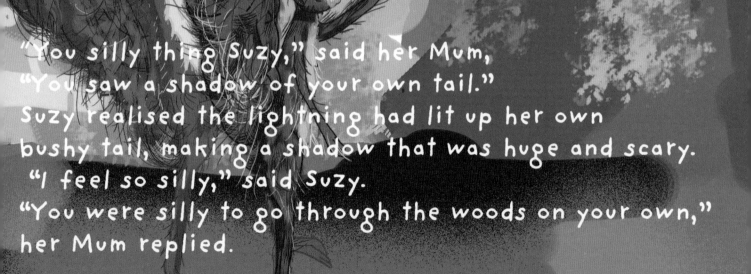

"You silly thing Suzy," said her Mum,
"You saw a shadow of your own tail."
Suzy realised the lightning had lit up her own
bushy tail, making a shadow that was huge and scary.
"I feel so silly," said Suzy.
"You were silly to go through the woods on your own,"
her Mum replied.

"Sorry," Suzy said, "I had to take a short cut...",
"Because you didn't leave enough time to get home."
Her Mum replied, "Just like you didn't leave enough
time to clean your bowl and spoon." Suzy had learned
her lesson.

Always do your work and don't go to

scary places **Alone.**

A Scary Tale

First Edition 27/8/2021

About The Creators

David Kline has a passion for storytelling. He is an award winning filmmaker with a background in scriptwriting. He has also worked extensively in education and believes children's stories should be fun, engaging and enlightening, supporting learning about one's self and the world about us.

Dave Roberts relishes using pictures to enhance stories. With over 20 years experience in graphic design he has honed his craft via business and education. He believes everyone can benefit from children's literature, through stories that can shape and define our lives and those around us.

Printed in Great Britain
by Amazon

87371915R00022